The
MAGIC WELL

BY MAIDA SILVERMAN
ILLUSTRATED BY MANUEL BOIX

SIMON AND SCHUSTER BOOKS FOR YOUNG READERS
Published by Simon & Schuster Inc./New York

SIMON AND SCHUSTER
BOOKS FOR YOUNG READERS
Simon & Schuster Building, Rockefeller Center,
1230 Avenue of the Americas, New York, New York 10020

SIMON AND SCHUSTER BOOKS FOR YOUNG READERS
is a trademark of Simon & Schuster Inc.
Manufactured in the United States of America

10 9 8 7 6 5 4 3 2 1

LIBRARY OF CONGRESS CATALOGING-IN-PUBLICATION DATA
Silverman, Maida.   The magic well.
Summary: Lured to the fairy world by the promise of a playmate, a young girl soon
tires of her new life and tries to find a way to escape the fairies' power and return
home to her mother. [1. Fairies—Fiction.   2. Mothers and daughters—Fiction.]
I. Boix, Manuel, ill.   II. Title.
PZ7.S5863Mag   [E]—dc19   89-5980
ISBN 0-617-67885-X

For Abigail
and in memory of Sylvia Markham
—MS

For Anna and Nelo
—MB

 N A TIME LONG AGO, when fairies could mingle with mortal folk, a little girl named Janet lived with her mother in a cottage at the edge of an ancient forest. As always in summer, Janet awoke at the sound of the earliest bird of morning. She hurried to the room where her mother slept, but her mother was not there. Janet quickly dressed and ran into the garden.

"Mother, are you here?" she called.

The sun winked through the tall trees, and the trees waved their branches, but only the birds answered Janet. Slowly and sadly, she went back to the cottage.

"Mother has gone away again to work on our neighbor's farm," she told her littlest doll. "I wish I were big enough to help, so I could go with her."

Janet set the mother doll and her three doll children in a circle on the floor. She brought ferns and oak leaves for dishes, and hazelnuts for food. Then she sat down next to the mother doll and ate her own breakfast of bread and cheese.

"Mother doll, you never leave your children," said Janet. "I wish you were alive, and the doll children too, so you could talk and play with me."

When Janet's mother returned, the sun was high above the trees. Janet ran to greet her.

"Oh, mother," she cried, "I'm so glad you are here! The wild dewberries must be ripe. Can we go and pick them together?"

"Certainly," her mother answered. "And we need more twigs for our fire. We'll gather them also." She put her arms around Janet. "I miss you when I am away. You always wait for me so patiently."

The dewberries grew deep in the forest under beech and
holly trees. Janet and her mother filled the basket with the
sweet purple fruit and gathered twigs of alder and birch. As
Janet knelt to tie her sash around the twigs, she saw a glimmer
of white and heard a rustling sound.

"Mother, look," she whispered.

A pair of wood doves fluttered in the branches of a tree.

"How beautiful they are!" said Janet. "I would want to be
a wood dove, if ever I were a bird."

Soon the basket of dewberries was full. The bundle of
twigs grew heavy. Janet and her mother had walked far, and
were glad when they came to a cool spring. A ring of mossy
stones enclosed it and made a deep well of the waters. Beside
the well, a beautiful rosebush bloomed.

Janet's mother sat down to rest, and Janet gathered roses
for a garland. But when she came back, her arms filled with
flowers, her mother had fallen asleep.

Janet sat down beside her and wove a garland by herself. After a while, she became aware of someone calling to her. Janet looked up and saw a beautiful lady sitting at the well.

"Your garland is lovely," the lady said. "Won't you bring it to me?"

"Oh, yes," Janet answered. She did not notice that a rose had fallen beside her sleeping mother and was left behind.

"Who are you?" asked Janet as she held out the flowers. "Where have you come from? There was no one here before."

The lady took the garland and placed it on Janet's head.

"I am Queen of the Fairies," she answered. "You summoned me from the well when you picked my roses. Look into the well now, and tell me what you see."

Janet bent over the rim of stones, but it was not her reflection crowned with roses that she saw. Instead, she saw a marvelous place, where a child waved and beckoned to her.

"The spring is magical," the lady said. "The well is magical, too. It is a window, and a passage between the mortal world and the world where fairies dwell."

"If only the little girl I saw was here to play with me," Janet sighed.

"That little girl is my own child," the Queen replied. "Will you come with me, and be her playmate?"

"Oh, yes," cried Janet. "I've wished for a playmate for such a long time!"

"You are a mortal child," the Queen replied. "You must take food and drink before you come with me."

Janet was hungry. She gladly ate the sweet cakes the lady gave her, and she drank water from the magic well. The Fairy Queen wrapped Janet in her shimmering silver cape.

"Come with me now," she said.

Janet turned back to look at her mother. It seemed to her that the forest, bright before, was suddenly darker. She could barely see her mother, still sleeping beneath a tree.

"You shall return before she wakes," the Fairy Queen promised, and she put her arms around Janet. "You have drunk our water and eaten our food," she whispered. "Now you are one of us!" Holding Janet tightly, she slipped over the rim of the well and they disappeared into the water.

When Janet's mother awoke, the sun had nearly set. She was all alone in the forest. She called Janet's name, but no one answered. She searched for her, but in vain. All she found was the rose that had fallen from Janet's garland. Tenderly, she picked it up and kissed it. Then she gathered up the bundle of twigs and the basket of dewberries. In despair, she retured to the cottage.

For a while, Janet was very happy. The Queen gave her a fine green dress, golden shoes, and a red cap for her hair. The Queen's child was her playmate, and other fairy children joined in their games.

Janet was not aware of the passing of time, for nothing changed in the world where the fairies lived. New plants never sprouted. Leaves never fell from the trees. Fruit was always ripe and flowers reappeared as soon as they were picked, just as if they had never been picked at all.

Rain never fell, wind never blew. There was neither sun, nor moon, nor stars. There was only an endless twilight of grey and gold.

In the mortal world, summer had changed into autumn. Janet's mother grieved for her lost daughter. She kept the rose, and kissed it each evening before going to sleep and again when she woke in the morning.

The rose bloomed on, long past the time it should have withered. Janet's mother kept the flower always near. "You are linked to the life of my child," she said. "As long as you remain alive, I know that in some faraway place, all is well with Janet."

One day, Janet sought out the Fairy Queen where she sat beneath an alder tree. "I would like to go back to the forest," she said. "My mother will be very frightened if I am not there when she wakes up."

"Many days and weeks have passed in the mortal world," the Queen told her. "Your mother has long since awakened and left the forest. She has probably even forgotten you."

"Mother would never forget me," Janet answered.

"I shall let you see your mother," said the Fairy Queen. "But she shall not see you, for I will make you invisible. And if you do not return to us, you shall stay invisible forever!"

Janet was grieved by the Queen's cruel trick, but as she made her way through the forest, she thought of a way for her mother to know her. She gathered twigs of alder and birch. Soon her arms were full.

When she came to the cottage, her mother was sleeping. Janet gently kissed her. She found her sash, tied the twigs, and laid them in front of the fireplace. She arranged the doll family in a circle, and put hazelnuts on oak-leaf plates in front of each one. Then she took the rose from her mother's side and laid it in the middle of the circle.

"If only I could stay here till mother wakes," she told her littlest doll. "But if I do, the Fairy Queen will keep me invisible forever!" So Janet hurried back to the magic well and returned to the fairies' world.

When her mother woke, she found the twigs tied with Janet's sash, the circle of dolls, and the rose. She saw that Janet had been there, and rejoiced that her child was indeed alive. But she was sad as she cradled the rose in her hands. "Shall I ever see my dear child," she wondered, "and have her back again?"

One day, the Fairy Queen's child came to Janet with great
glee. "Tonight is Halloween," she said, "the night of the Fairy
Ride. Once every seven years, we ride through the forests of the
mortal world. You shall go with us, and then we'll be playmates
forever, for you'll never leave our world again!"

When the fairy child had gone away, Janet thought a long
while. She knew she must think of a way to escape on the night
of the Fairy Ride. If only her mother could rescue her!

Janet went once again to the Fairy Queen. "When the Fairy
Ride is over, I will stay with the fairies forever. May I visit my
mother one last time?"

"You may," said the Queen.

"And may I go as a white wood dove?"

"Yes," the Queen replied. "But you must not linger, for if you do, you'll stay a wood dove always!" She clapped her hands three times, and changed Janet into a bird.

Janet sped through the forest on wood dove's wings. When she reached the cottage, a window was open and she flew inside. Her mother was sitting near the fireplace. The bird fluttered above her head for a moment, then took the rose in its beak and flew out the window.

"Janet! Janet!" her mother cried, for she realized the wood dove was her daughter. She ran from the cottage and followed the bird into the forest.

The bird flew to the ring of mossy stones and dropped the rose into the water. When Janet's mother reached the well, the wood dove was gone. Floating round and round on the water's surface was the rose. Far below, she saw the fairies' world, and Janet, who spoke to her:

"The night to come is Halloween, the night of the Fairy Ride. The Fairy Court will ride through the forest and come to the well, and I will be with them," she said.

"Oh mother, you must pull me away from them as I ride by. You must hold me tight and not let me go, or the fairies will keep me forever!"

A sudden breeze ruffled the water and the picture vanished. Janet's mother reached out toward the rose, but as she touched it, it sank beneath her hand and disappeared into the well.

Halloween night was moonless and dark. Janet's mother returned to the well in the forest and hid herself behind a rowan tree. A chill wind rose, and the branches trembled. After a while, the sigh of the wind gave way to the sounds of unearthly music and the jingling of bells. The sounds grew louder as, riding on horses, the fairy procession appeared through the trees.

The Ride was led by the Fairy Queen. Her lords and ladies came after. Next came a tumbling, mumbling crowd of imps, hobgoblins and elves. Some of the fairies blew horns and

panpipes. Others shook tambourines. Silver bells jingled on horses' bridles and flickering will-o'-the-wisps cast eerie light. Janet's mother waited, and watched as they passed by.

At last the fairy children came. Janet was with them, riding a fine white horse. Her mother ran up and pulled her away, and held Janet tight in her arms.

The Fairy Queen gave a cry of rage. She clapped her hands, as did all the court, and the will-o'-the-wisps whirled around them. And as they clapped, Janet changed shape in her mother's arms.

They changed her into a sharp-scaled snake that writhed
and twisted and tried to bite, then a salamander, whose tail
lashed like a whip. They changed her into a bear with a
hundred sharp teeth, and a lion whose mane was sharp spikes.

They made her an eagle with feathers like thorns, and a wolf
with a hundred sharp claws. They changed her into an eel with
needle fins, and a toad whose feet pulled at her mother's hair.

But Janet's mother was not afraid, and she clung very tight to them all.

"You shall let go of her now!" cried the Queen.

She changed Janet into a child made of iron that glowed red

hot, as if on fire. This was the hardest of all to hold, but her mother clasped it tight.

The Fairy Queen wailed loudly as the iron child melted away and turned into Janet herself. She was safe in her mother's arms.

Golden rays of the rising sun shone brightly through trees and branches. Halloween was over. The Fairy Ride faded into the mists that rose from the ring of stones. The Queen reached out and tried to grasp Janet, but she had escaped from the fairies.

Janet held her mother's hand as they walked home through the forest. They turned to look back at the magic well. A playful breeze blew the petals from the last of the roses. They swirled and fluttered up in the air, and then fell into the water.